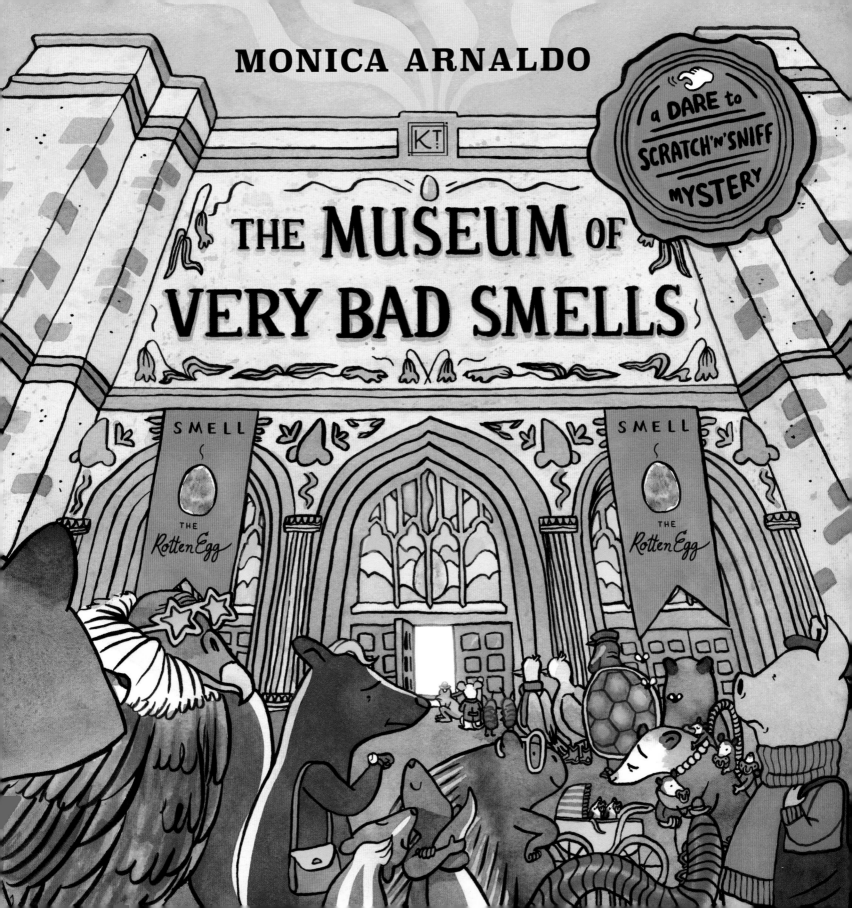

For all the brave and brilliant children who dare to sniff.
And for the parents who deal with Very Bad Smells daily: I'm sorry (and here is one more).
—M.A.

Katherine Tegen Books is an imprint of HarperCollins Publishers.

The Museum of Very Bad Smells
Copyright © 2024 by Monica Arnaldo
For information address HarperCollins Children's Books, a division of HarperCollins Publishers, 195 Broadway, New York, NY 10007.
www.harpercollinschildrens.com

Library of Congress Control Number: 2023944245
ISBN 978-0-06-327144-9

The artist used acrylic ink and watercolor to create the illustrations for this book.
Typography by Amy Ryan
24 25 26 27 28 IMG 10 9 8 7 6 5 4 3 2 1
First Edition